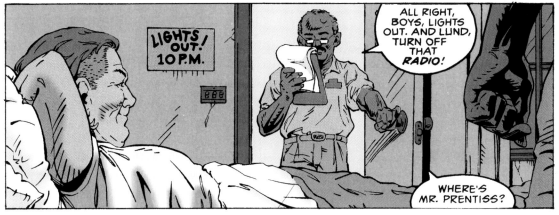

LIGHTS! OUT! 10 P.M.

ALL RIGHT, BOYS, LIGHTS OUT. AND LUND, TURN OFF THAT *RADIO!*

WHERE'S MR. PRENTISS?

-- SNICKER --

UH, HE'S PROBABLY OUT WATERIN' A TREE.

CAP, THAT TRUE?

UH -- GEE, MORTY. WE KINDA SENT HIM OUT ON A *WAMPUS HUNT.*

YOU *DOPE!* NEXT TIME WE SEND *YOU* ON THE HUNT!

WRMF

BOYS, BOYS. ANDREW IS *NEW* HERE. HE DOESN'T KNOW THESE WOODS LIKE YOU DO.

WHO KNOWS *WHAT* HE MIGHT RUN INTO..?

... AND FOR ALL YOU *U.F.O. WATCHERS,* THERE'VE BEEN SEVERAL REPORTS ABOUT *STRANGE LIGHTS* APPEARING OVER THE SOUTH WOODS...

HOLD ON, GUYS! I'M ON MY WAY!

JUST DON'T TURN OFF THOSE FLASH--

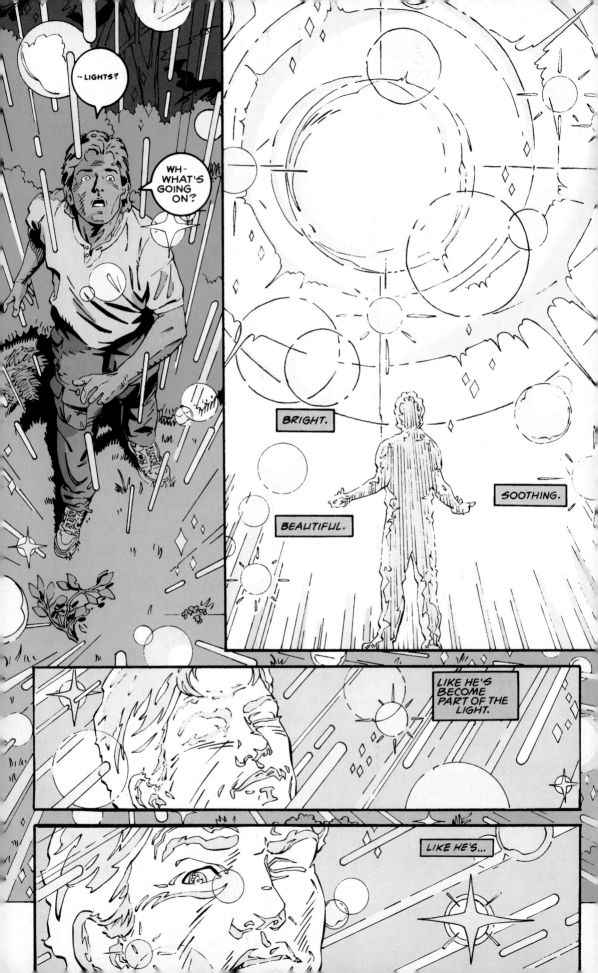

WGKX NEWS: A RIOT HAS BROKEN OUT AT THE *COOL SPRINGS GALLERY MALL.* OFFICIALS CLAIM IT WAS STARTED BY A GANG DRESSED IN HALLOWE'EN COSTUMES.

WELL?

LET'S DO IT!

UM, GUS... DO YOU THINK I COULD COME BACK LATER AND TALK ABOUT THIS "*FAITH*" THING?

IF NICK DOESN'T KILL ME, THAT IS.

THE ONLY CLOCK THAT'S GETTIN' CLEANED IS *NICK'S. I* HAVE FAITH IN YOU.

WE'LL TALK WHEN YOU GET BACK!

YOU'VE GOT THE JACKET I WORE WHEN I RODE WITH THE *SENTINELS.* HERE'S THE *HELMET.* SAVED MY LIFE.

YOU SURE YOU'RE READY?

NO. BUT I'M SURE I'M GOING.